DISCARD

WIENER WOLF

Jeff Crosby

Disney • Hyperion Books
New York

For information address Disney • Hyperion Books, 114 Fifth Avenue, New York, New York 10011-5690.
First Edition

10 9 8 7 6 5 4 3 2 1
F850-6835-5-11032
Printed in Singapore
ISBN 978-14231-3983-6
Visit www.hyperionbooksforchildren.com

Wiener Dog seldom wagged his tail anymore.

His toy had lost its squeak.

He was hungry for something new.

Life with Granny had become too tame.

Until…

He hightailed it out of there

and hitched a ride.

He took to the wilderness and nosed around, looking for...

Wiener Dog understood.

He became...

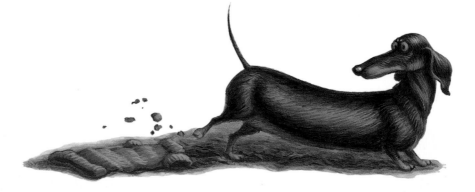

Wiener Wolf!

He had a new backyard

and a new water dish

and new squeaky toys.

Wiener Wolf
answered the
call of the wild!

Arrrrooooooooooooooooo!

That night he dreamed.

The next day began
with hide-and-seek,

followed by a game of chase.

YIKES!

Wiener Wolf suddenly felt like Wiener Dog,

and Wiener Dog belonged at home

He welcomed his old dish,
old yard, and old squeaky toy.

Granny even knit him a
new sweater.

But Granny knew Wiener Dog also needed...

And he got them.

[15]